A RIP SQUEAK® BOOK

Rip Squeak and His Friends

Written by **Susan Yost-Filgate**

Illustrated by **Leonard Filgate**

RIP SQUEAK, INC. ~ SAN LUIS OBISPO, CALIFORNIA

For Jessica

PUBLISHED BY RIP SQUEAK, INC.
840 CAPITOLIO WAY, SUITE B
SAN LUIS OBISPO, CALIFORNIA 93405

This book was originally published as Rip Squeak and His Friends © 2000, 2005 by Rip Squeak, Inc.
All rights reserved. This edition is published under license from Rip Squeak, Inc.
Any use or sublicense of this book in any format or matter must be approved in writing by
Raven Tree Press, a Division of Delta Systems Co., Inc.,
1400 Miller Parkway, McHenry, IL 60050-7030
www.raventreepress.com

RIP SQUEAK®, JESSE & BUNNY™, ABBEY™, EURIPIDES™, and
RIP SQUEAK AND HIS FRIENDS™ are trademarks of Rip Squeak, Inc.

Library of Congress Control Number: 2005926909

ISBN-13: 978-1-934960-40-0

Edited by Lee Cohen ∾ Designed by Willabel L. Tong

Don't miss the other books in this series:
rip squeak and his friends ∾ the treasure ∾ the adventure ∾ find the magic ∾ the surprise party

To learn more about other products from Rip Squeak, visit
www.RipSqueak.com

Printed in China
10 9 8 7 6 5 4 3 2 1
Revised Edition

Free activities for this book are available at www.raventreepress.com.

A RIP SQUEAK® BOOK

Rip Squeak and His Friends

Written by **Susan Yost-Filgate**

Illustrated by **Leonard Filgate**

Raven Tree Press
A Division of Delta Systems Co., Inc.

WHEN the humans left the cottage, it was *soooo* quiet.

Rip Squeak was busy writing down his great adventures. Suddenly, he heard a strange noise. His sister heard it, too. Quietly, they moved toward the kitchen.

"Be brave," Rip said. He peeked around the corner—only to hear the sound every mouse dreads…

Meeeooooowwww!

A kitten was curled up on the floor in the kitchen. She was crying.

"I'm all alone," whimpered the kitten. "My family left without me."

"You're not alone," Rip told her. "We will be your friends. My name is Rip Squeak, and this is my sister, Jesse."

"I'm Abbey," said the kitten.

Together the new friends raced to the garden. They spent hours playing games, telling stories and chasing butterflies.

"It looks like rain," said Abbey after a while. "I hate getting wet. Let's go inside." Rip and Jesse climbed on Abbey and the kitten raced back into the cottage.

But Jesse liked the rain. Soon she was outside again, happily splashing in the puddles. She didn't even notice a tomcat creeping toward her. Rip and Abbey tried to warn her through the window, but Jesse couldn't hear them.

Then, she saw the tomcat. She bravely pushed her umbrella in his face.

All at once, a strange creature appeared, wearing a big hat and cape.
He waved a sword, and the bad cat ran away.

Jesse ran to Rip. "That tomcat almost got me, but I fought back!" she cried. "You sure did!" answered Rip, hugging her close.

The stranger took a deep bow. "Hello. My name is Euripides." He told them he was an actor. He explained how acting is about using your imagination. Then, he began to tell the friends grand stories.

"Oh my, look at the time," Euripides said. "I'm off to the theater! Don't forget to use your imagination!" he called as he was leaving.

The friends weren't sure what to do next. So they made popcorn, told silly jokes, and played hide–and–seek. But the kitten looked sad. Rip knew she was missing her family.

"Let's play some music," he suggested. "Music always makes me happy."

Soon, they were all dancing and laughing. Mom and Dad Squeak heard the sounds and came into the living room to watch.

THUMP went something in the kitchen. Everyone stopped dancing. "I hope I haven't startled you," said a voice from the other room.

In hopped Euripides, right onto the piano. He began to sing in a booming voice. Rip Squeak danced on the piano keys.

Abbey was so happy! "Now I have a surprise for all of you," she purred.

"A surprise?!" exclaimed Euripides. "Then I must change into something more suitable."

Euripides returned in a brilliant new costume. "Are you ready for the surprise?" Abbey asked. The friends nodded. With a grand sweep of her tail, Abbey opened a door.

The friends could not believe their eyes. "So many toys!" squealed Jesse.

"I wanted to share this special place with you. You are the best friends any cat could wish for," Abbey purred. The friends thanked her, and everyone started to play.

There were toys of every kind—big toys and tiny toys, soft toys and noisy toys, worn toys and new toys. Rip and Jesse found a puppet that looked just like Euripides in his new costume. "We've discovered a whole new world right under our noses!" Rip said.

Abbey was so pleased that her friends were
having fun. She even tried to show off on a ball
she'd found.

Everyone played and played until they were too tired to play anymore. Then Abbey curled up on a pillow, and the friends nestled against her. The sound of Abbey's soft purring made them all feel sleepy.

"It sure is great to make new friends," thought Rip, as his eyes closed slowly. Today had changed everything. Soon, he was dreaming of the new adventures tomorrow would bring.